This Christmas

Harper Rae James

Cover design: Harper Rae James

First edition 2025

Printed in the United States of America

ISBN: 979-8-9918148-5-0

Dedication

T O ANYONE WHO BELIEVES in the magic of Christmas… may your nights only be silent after you've screamed his name.

Cheers to being on the naughty list, for all the Christmases to come.

Trigger Warnings

With holiday mischief,

Harper Rae

Playlist

FOR AN IMMERSIVE READING experience, download this playlist on Spotify.

Sleigh my Name

"Sleigh my name, sleigh my name when no one is around you…"

-Withers

Ana

"**I**'M HIDING IN THE goddamn pantry, Blake."

Hiding.

In a fucking pantry.

Instead of being out there with all of our guests, I'm a coward in the dark corner on FaceTime with my best friend.

This might actually be my lowest of lows.

"What the hell are you waiting for?" Blake's voice echoes through the small space as I stare at her on my phone screen.

"This feels ridiculous. We're married, have two kids, and let me remind you, we're at his company holiday party."

"He's the owner, Ana. No one gives a shit what he does," she reminds me. "Make the best of this weekend while you can."

The pantry is tucked off the main kitchen of the mountain cabin Knox rented for his company holiday retreat, so it's only a matter of time before someone—hopefully, my husband—notices the light and comes in to find me in this ridiculous position, crouched on the floor.

My husband.

The most amazing man I know.

I'm just relighting the fire, I remind myself.

The fire that's still there, between us, smoldering in the way we lock eyes over a mountain of dishes, in the accidental brush of hands reaching for the same bottle of dish soap. But we're tired. So fucking tired that even a kiss feels like a never ending 7th inning stretch. By the time we hit the pillow, we're too exhausted to do anything but roll to our separate sides of the bed and pass out. Every now and then, I will catch him staring at me like he's remembering who I am, like he wants to devour me, and I can't help but smile. We may not be setting the sheets on fire as often as we'd like, but at least we're still kinda *sparking*… right?

I peek through the small crack I left myself and look out into the sea of people. The room is dimly lit, wrapped in the glow of soft string of lights draped across the wooden ceiling beams and coiled around the staircase railing. The fireplace crackles steadily, casting a flickering amber light as it moves lazily across the room. There is a slightly imperfect Christmas tree standing near the window with soft Christmas music flowing from the speakers.

The room's crowded, but cozy. People fill every corner. There are clients, investors, and a few foundation members present.

Knox opened a youth training facility, a dream of his we have been collectively working on for years. He goes to the facility to oversee everything while I run all things PR, letting my marketing degree come in handy. I absolutely love it. I get to work from home and stay close to our children, Riker and Rory, at the same time. We have a new nanny we share with the neighbors, allowing me to work from home and it's the best thing we've done for our family in so many ways.

"Well," Blake cuts in, stealing my attention away from my racing thoughts, "Get your fine ass out there and have some fun with your husband, Ana. Leaving the kids with the nanny for the weekend doesn't happen, well… ever!"

She's right. I can't remember the last time Knox and I had a night alone together. I'm not even sure I remember what it's like to have an orgasm that's not muffled by a pillow, if we even make it that far.

"Okay, I'll call you tomorrow." My voice is shaky, and my palms are sweaty. I'm losing confidence in my plan… well, Blake's plan, that is.

"Ana, toys and games can be fun. Trust me. He will love it. We picked the best items from my inventory." Blake owns a bookstore complete with a bar and adult toy shop, and she convinced me to take products for this weekend. She gives me one more reassuring smile before ending our FaceTime.

Exhaling loud enough for the sounds to filter through the small space of the pantry, I grab my glass of champagne and the box of crackers I "came in here to get" so I could refill the tray on the counter. I am careful despite my shaky hand as I slide the tiny, red iridescent envelope into my bra for safekeeping.

As I walk out of the kitchen, I am met with the judgmental gaze of a few baseball moms standing on the other side of the small island in the middle of the kitchen.

I would stop and assess my dress, cleavage, and makeup if I hadn't just had Blake give me a once-over through the screen. Odds are, this is the gaggle of women eye-fucking my husband every chance they get, and they are just picking me apart to make themselves feel better.

As I walk by them, I stand up a little taller and pop out my chest a little further just for show.

Jokes on them, because the only one fucking him tonight is me.

He instantly notices my entrance. The feeling of hunger in his eyes is clear across the space between us. When I look up, I'm met with his emerald gaze only on me. I see hunger in his eyes, and it pushes the thought of the women near me aside as if nobody else exists. There he is. *My man.* Standing across the room, half shadowed by the glow from the string lights, and a soda water forgotten in his hand.

He doesn't look away. Of course he doesn't. It's not his style, and I don't want him to.

His eyes roam slowly, heavily across my body like he's stripping back every layer without touching a thing. As if he knows exactly what his look is doing to me and has no intention of stopping. The intoxicating heat pouring from him feels like I'm standing here in nothing but a secret. My skin is flushed, cheeks warm and breath caught low in my chest, like it always is under his stare.

He doesn't smile. Just tilts his head the slightest bit, with all the ease and confidence in the world, like he did the night we met, letting me know exactly what he's thinking. And when he runs his tongue over his lip ring, I'm done for. Lord help me, I couldn't look away even if I wanted to.

But deep inside, I just want him to see me. Not the mother of his kids. Just me.

Knox

T HE PANTRY DOOR OPENED, and she emerged like a wet fucking dream. With her face glowing from the distant lights and a soft smile on her face, my mouth instantly went dry.

How is it, after two kids, sleeping next to her naked body for countless nights, and picking her hair out of the drain, she still makes me go fucking feral?

I want nothing more than to bend her over, slide her little red velvet dress up over her waist and fuck her until her hips bruise from me slamming them into the edge of the counter.

I want her smell, her taste, the feel of her skin to surround every bit of me.

I raise my hand in the air and summon her to me with a come-hither motion. The smirk crossing her face, her narrow pointed gaze and quirked lips, makes my dick twitch in my pants. Fuck, I love this woman.

She shifts, and to anyone else she appears to be adjusting her dress, but I know better. My girl is chasing friction, just enough to make the walk across the room bearable. Her panties are already soaked, I'm sure of it.

"Yes?" she asks when she reaches me. Her tone is flat, a mask covering the desire lying beneath.

"What do you think you're doing, Stitch?"

"Refilling the crackers."

"What's with the dress, babe?" She hates dresses. Other than our wedding, I can only recall one other time she wore one, and it was only for a few minutes before she changed.

"You don't like it?" She knows I do and is messing with me.

"I fucking love it. But I can tell you don't." I know she doesn't.

"I might," she tries to argue.

"You don't." It's a fact. One I'd bet on. All in, not a doubt in my mind.

"You don't want me in it?" she asks, playing coy with me.

"No," I give her a pointed smile. "I'd rather see it crumpled on the floor, but that's true for anything you wear."

"Hey, buddy," a loud voice interrupts, making Ana jump in surprise. I recognize the voice before I even turn around, and I want to kick his ass for interrupting this moment, but I cover my actual emotions with a friendly smile.

"Marcus, when did you get here?" Marcus is the investor I have been working with trying to get more equipment for the baseball facility. He's a nice enough guy, although he's blindly cock blocking me at the moment.

"Here." He offers me a beer.

"Thanks man, but I don't drink," I say, holding up my soda water. "But I'm sure my wife will enjoy it." Ana smiles, taking the beer and bringing it to her lips. Add that to the almost empty glass of champagne in her other hand, and she's going to be keyed up any moment.

I want my cock to be that fucking bottle, wrapped in her warm, wet mouth.

"Stitch, Marcus is the guy I was telling you about this morning, the one funding our new equipment. Marcus, this is my wife, Ana."

"It's nice to meet you." She smiles, but it's not her usual smile. She's nervous, though I'm not sure why. Ana was a bartender for years, and is great at making small talk with people. She never gets nervous around new people. She moves through conversations like a breeze through wind chimes. It's gentle, natural and leaves warmth in her wake. "I'm going to finish refilling the trays," she whispers the words to me as she leans in and kisses my cheek, and it's then I realize her voice is shaky.

Last time she was this nervous, I almost lost her.

As her lips meet my skin, I notice her pulling something out of her bra just before her hand slides into the back pocket of my pants.

I watch her as she walks away as I also reach into my pocket and feel something resembling a business card.

What the fuck?

I pull it out of my pocket to get a better look and find a small envelope.

Marcus and I shot the shit longer than I wanted. Every time I tried to close the conversation, he would start a new one. I nodded, laughed, adding nothing. The whole time, that damn envelope burned a hole in my pocket like a dare.

Shimmery, red, small.

I repeat these words curiously in my mind as Marcus talks, trying to decipher them.

It's just tucked there like it's meaningless. Just a small card in an envelope, my name scrawled across the front in handwriting I know too damn well.

I haven't opened it. Not yet. I can't. The last handwritten message I got from her changed the entire trajectory of our relationship.

But I *feel* it. The weight of it, ridiculous as it sounds. It's like it's alive. This tiny envelope rubs against my thigh, daring me to crack it open with every step I take, every club soda I pretend to enjoy. I keep reaching for it, fingers brushing the edge, tugging it out halfway before stuffing it right back in.

When Marcus excuses himself to use the restroom and refill his drink, I slip into the corner of the room quietly and unnoticed. Masked by the chatter and clinking glasses, I pause between heartbeats.

I look around for her, and each time I scan the room I come up empty, reminding me of the night we met. When I scan the room one last time, void of my girl, curiosity wins out, and I peel the envelope open.

As I read it, I realize she wasn't just nervous to give this because this is not something she would usually do; she's nervous to have me see that she's missing something.

And that something is *me*.

You know that saying? Sometimes the truth hurts? Yeah.

That doesn't even skim the surface of the truth bomb I just laid on myself, because, the truth is, sometimes I forget to look. Not because I don't care, but because I assume she'll always be there.

Anticipation and regret sit side by side, as I read the note she left in my pocket.

> *I hope you've been a good boy, but I have a feeling you've been extra naughty. Lucky for you, there's still time to make the nice list. Ready for a little holiday fun?*
>
> *Here's your first clue, hotshot:*
>
> *"I'm where you hang your hat, but not where you lay your head. I'll keep things warm, but don't expect to find me on the bed."*
>
> *I'll be waiting. And who knows, maybe you'll be the one to "sleigh my name tonight".*
>
> *-Stitch*

Have Yourself a Merry Little Lit-mas

"From now on, our troubles will be out of sight…"
-Michael Buble

Ana

THE ROOM IS PITCH black, except for the glow of the Christmas lights shining in the small window in the mudroom's corner. Lights that illuminate the small cooler bag Blake sent with me. Because, fuck, the woman plans for chaos.

"I'm perched on the dryer in a velvet dress like a damn Christmas cliché, waiting for my man. It's ridiculous. And I love it."

Because, who am I?

Ana Fucking Reed, that's who.

A horny mom of two, who just wants as many stolen moments with her husband as she can take without feeling guilty about it.

I lingered in the kitchen, mingled with the few wives I know, and watched him fidget in anticipation and nervousness. The last time I slid him a little note, it contained bombshell upon bombshell. I saw the curiosity turn to panic in his expression and understood the connection between the past and present. Knox is so easy to read, and stress, yeah, he wears it on his face like a fan in the stands during a losing streak, hoping for a miracle.

Once he finally opened it, I casually made my way to the mudroom at the end of the hallway just off the kitchen. Away from the crowd, tucked in a dark little corner of the cottage we will call home for the weekend.

Could I have waited until all his guests left? Yes. Would it have been as fun? No.

It's madness, I know. But I'm too far in; I can't stop. The way he looks at me, it's like a dare wrapped in a promise. Every glance sends heat rushing through my core, every brush of skin feels like a spark to dry kindling. It's forbidden. Reckless. I want that fire, need that fire. It's what I'm chasing.

Suddenly he comes stalking through the door, and the sight of his enormous erection pushing on his pants, just for me, is the first thing I notice.

"This," he says, raising the card in the air, "is fucking genius." His voice is dripping with desire, but his eyes always speak the truth. His mask is on. He doesn't want me to know he saw the truth behind this game.

He pauses for a second, but in an instant, like any man would do in this position, he pushes the emotion hiding in his eyes aside, and in one swift motion, he's on me.

Snaking his arm around my leg, wrapping it around his waist as he swiftly readjusts me on the dryer to make room for him between my legs. He peppers kisses down my neck and chest, leaving marks I'm sure by the pressure and force delivering them.

"I fucking want you right now, so fucking bad." His words tumble out of him with a deep, raspy drawl.

"You only get my mouth at the moment." My response is quick and breathy with a smirk that promises more later.

"I love when you take charge. How exactly do I get your mouth, baby? Your lips on mine, or do I have other options?"

"You can have it however you want," I say, already knowing and ready for his response.

"I want it wrapped around my dick, sliding up and down, hitting the back of your throat." He thinks he's making a request, but my hands were already working his buckle. There is nothing I crave more than the salty taste of him on my tongue.

"I want you to come down my throat," I smile at the fire in his gaze as it's so apparent, even in the dimly lit space. I never talk to him like this, but it's making me feel more alive than I have in a while.

"Dirty girl. What if I want to come inside you? Fill you with another Knox Jr." His words are not a question. We want more kids, and we learned about Knox's little pregnancy kink with Rory. Me carrying our baby is a turn-on for us both.

"Later. We're just getting started," I promise, sealing it with a kiss, just before I slide off the dryer.

"Fuck," he groans, moving back to give me space. My movements are slow. Calculated. Each sway of my hips and bite of my lip is intentional as I drop to my knees before him.

I lick the length of his hard cock, making a little circle around the tip before sliding it deep into my throat. I get a little ambitious, and when he hits the back of my throat, it constricts.

"Ana, fuck. Don't do that or I'll lose it before I've even savored it." He looks down at me, placing his hand beneath my jaw.

The room is dark, so I'm not surprised by the delay in him noticing my lips painted cherry red. When he sees them, his eyes follow them up and down his length.

"Stitch," he whispers, with a hint of desire coating his words as he smears the red lipstick with his index finger.

With his one word of approval, my nickname, I close my lips around him, painting a perfect red ring at his base. His eyes roll back, and he grips the back of my hair, fucking my mouth as fast as he can, pumping in and out until I'm gasping for air.

The sound of my ragged breath fills the room, and I open for him as hot spurts of come coat my lips and tongue.

I swallow every last drop and lick my lips clean before standing.

I've barely caught my breath before he spins me around so my hips are flush with the dryer.

"Knox," I whimper.

"Anabelle." His tone is firm with a hint of a warning. He uses my full name only when his control is paper thin. He kicks my feet apart. "Spread your legs."

I do as I'm told, and the reward for my obedience is a smack across my ass while he hikes my dress to my waist. It's only then that he realizes I'm bare with nothing between us.

"Where are your panties, Ana?"

"I lost them. Guess you'll have to find them."

Knox

"YOU ARE DRIPPING," I say as I run my tongue up her inner thigh, chasing the trail of arousal rolling down her leg. "What are the rules, baby?"

"Only your mouth," she says between pants.

"Fingers?" I ask, wanting to clarify exactly what she wants.

"Only. Your. Mouth. Knox."

I could push her, argue she had a bratty tone, but no fun would come of that. She's in charge, and I love it.

I want to spread her open, see the pale pink of her pussy shimmering in the soft glow of the lights fluttering in from the window. I want to explore all of her, admire her piercing that I love so much, but over my fucking dead body will I complain about tasting her instead. No, I'm going to fucking feast.

Deciding against this angle with the restrictions, I spin her back around and lift her back onto the dryer.

I settle on my knees and use my chin to push, making room for myself between her sweet legs. The shifting of her weight creates a squeaking sound as her skin slides across the cool metal of the dryer.

I roll my tongue through her opening, tasting her before taking a moment to admire her. The sight of her piercing glistening is my favorite sight. I gently pull it between my teeth and then glide it under my tongue, creating pressure on her clit exactly how she likes it.

She looks incredible, her porcelain skin a burst of sunlight in the dark laundry room. Her dark hair blends in with the shadows as it cascades down her body, matching the dark mahogany of the cabinets hung overhead.

"You always taste so fucking good."

Her body is something I've taken great time and dedication in learning over the years. I've memorized every inch of her skin, and every reaction to my touch. I know her rhythm, like the perfect swing of a bat, smooth and precise. I hit it just right every time.

But right now, I want to savor her, explore, and learn something new.

"Knox, right there," she pants, and I lean into the motion of my mouth on her. Devouring her like I need my next breath.

"Fuck this, babe. I need my hands, just to hold you open, I promise." I'll respect her rules, but I need to make this as good for her as she has for me.

When she doesn't protest, I place my fingers on her, spreading her open, admiring the pink of her skin as it glistens against her metal piercing. Wanting something different, I use my fingers to push the skin surrounding her clit away and suction my lips there. I suck her clit and piercing into my mouth, rolling them between my lips while changing the pressure from soft to more intense. I suck and massage her with my mouth, with all of my focus on her as I do it. Watching her eyes roll back in her head as she peers down at me, her legs shaking. Her chest gets blotchy, her breathing shallow. She tangles her hands in my hair, pushing me into her, like I had done with her just minutes before.

She comes undone on my mouth while her body goes limp on top of the dryer.

"Holy shit," she pants. "That was incredible."

She readjusts her dress and runs her fingers through her hair. I watch her intently as I refasten my belt and tuck in my shirt.

How the fuck did I get so fucking lucky?

She leans against the dryer, breathless, lips parted. I wipe my mouth with the back of my hand and grin up at her. "Still only my mouth, right?"

"Nice try," she says with a smile, attempting to smooth the wrinkles on my shirt and fix my tangled hair. "You're a mess, babe."

"I don't give a shit." I smirk.

She hands me a stick of gum from her purse hanging on a hook nearby.

I give her a sideways glance. "I don't want that."

"Knox?" She scrunches her brow.

"Baby, I want your taste on my tongue and smell on my face all night."

"Knox."

"No, Ana, I. Don't. Give. A. Fuck." I kiss her forehead and turn towards the door.

"Oh, wait." She moves to a small cooler bag on the floor by the coat rack and pulls out two cans.

Merry Lit-mas is scrolled across both cans.

"What's this?"

"Blake gave them to me. She got a free case with the order she received from the Sensual Lifestyle vendor she orders from for L&L. They're an aphrodisiac drink. It's supposed to increase arousal and send you into a fuzzy, lust induced state."

She assesses my reaction before she continues, "It's all natural, no stimulants or alcohol. I checked."

I love how diligent she is in her efforts to accommodate my sobriety, but right now it's the least of my worries.

"You want me to walk around with a hard-on?"

"That's what your waistband is for," she teases.

"Fair," I shake my head, taking one can from her.

We cheers and each chug down our can of the fizzy drink. Tiny bubbles and a light cranberry cinnamon flavor dance across my taste buds.

I inspect the can one more time before throwing it in the trash can.

"These are pretty fucking good. We might need to order more of these… if they work."

Do You Hear What I Hear?

"Do you know what I know?"

-Pentatonix and Whitney Huston

Ana

T HE ROOM SWIRLS AROUND, light flickering in the corner of my eye, the cadence mimicking the throb of my clit between my legs. Sweat traces down my hairline as I talk to a few of the moms, and I can't help but wipe it as it drips down my brow.

"Are you okay?" Winni asks.

"Fine, why?" My words are sharp, and I can't stand still.

"You keep fidgeting, and looking around the room like you're either extremely uncomfortable or hiding some big secret. Plus, there is sweat trickling down your face, sweetie. Are you feeling ok?"

No, there is a burn between my legs and it feels like frostbite under mittens, numb at first, then suddenly it hurts like hell. I need an orgasm more than I need my next breath. Every movement I make sends me to the edge of ecstasy, and my husband is nowhere to be found.

"Yeah, I just think I had too much caffeine today. You know how it is, right?" I ask with a chuckle, fake as the day is long. "We're away from the kids, so I overindulge in things I rarely indulge in." I chuckle again, but she doesn't buy it.

"Maybe you need to go lie down for a bit," she suggests.

Yeah, with my husband buried inside me.

Just then, I see Knox out of the corner of my eye, emerging from the bathroom, adjusting himself.

Motherfucker went and got himself off.

Cheater.

There's no time like the present to deliver my second note. He may have gotten his, but that asshole is going to give me mine.

I scurry across the room to where Knox is standing by the back door, looking at the light snow falling outside.

"You fucking little cheater," I scold in a whisper.

He turns with a curious glance, but it quickly shifts to concern.

"Shit, babe, are you okay? What? Y-you're dripping sweat."

"You just got yourself off, didn't you?" I whimper slightly between clenched teeth. I know he is the only one who can hear me. Especially with the Christmas music filtering through the space. He assesses me, not knowing how to play this.

"Ana, my dick hurt. It actually fucking hurt. It was not the normal arousal that builds with the anticipation of what's to come. Those drinks are not…" He looks around. "The shit they do to you is not normal," he whispers. "I had to. I didn't have a choice."

He gives me a sheepish smile. The look I give him in return is not one of amusement.

Oh… game on, motherfucker.

"Here," I say, handing him the next envelope, before storming off to the main suite.

I had plans for us. Plans that involved a wand Blake helped me pick out. It was going to be my next set of rules; we could only use the toy. Though I wasn't sure how I was going to manage that for him, given my lack of experience. Guess I don't have to worry about that now.

I close the bedroom door and shimmy out of my dress, sprawling myself across the bed in the gold lace set I put on after he left the mudroom. The note I left him was clear, so he shouldn't be long.

> *Where dreams begin and mornings start,*
>
> *A cozy room, the home's warm heart.*
>
> *Wrapped in blankets, soft and wide.*
>
> *Come find me where we both reside.*
>
> *-Stitch*

The air feels thick, like it's holding its breath. Every glance I take around the room is too sharp, the silence feeling too loud. All of my thoughts, dirty, delicious, frantic, hover just behind my clenched jaw, unsaid yet screaming inside my head. It's not anger between my legs, not yet, but it's a stirring that comes before a storm, tight and crackling, like static under your skin. I need to come so goddamn badly. If he doesn't hurry, he's going to miss it, and I won't even be sorry.

As if being summoned, he comes bursting in the door. "Ana, bab—" His words cut off when he sees me, and he hurries to close the door, looking behind him to ensure no one is there.

"Shit." He combs his fingers through his hair and stalks towards me, forgetting whatever it was he was about to say.

He reaches out to touch me, and I turn away from his touch.

"No, go sit in the chair, Knox." He looks around the room with a raise of his brow until he spots the armchair by the door.

"You want me way over there?" he asks with a hint of irritation.

"Yes."

"Ok…" His voice is definitely full of annoyance at my request, as if the notion of him sitting across the room from me sprawled out on the bed in lingerie is an absurdity. And in reality, I guess it is.

"You have been such a bad boy, Knox. I want you to stay there, hands where I can see them the entire time." My tone is playful and sultry, but he chuckles in response.

"What is so funny?" I ask, propping myself on one elbow so I can see him better.

"Who are you today?" He chuckles, and as he moves I see a dusting of red lipstick on his sleeve. We should probably be more careful so we don't give our secret away.

"Oh, sorry. If you don't want to spice things up, we can stop." I move to stand, but he quickly rises and makes it to me in two long strides.

Honestly, I don't know what got into me. Maybe it's the season. Maybe it's finally letting go. Either way, I'm not stopping.

"Fuck no," he pushes me back down to the bed and then returns to the armchair, placing his hands on his knees where I can see them.

"I was going to involve you," I say, holding up the wand and turning it on, "but then you went and cheated, chasing your own release, prematurely." I smile a wicked smile in his direction. "So, now, you get to watch."

"From *here*?" he asks, skeptical that I will actually make him stay there.

"Yes."

"What if I can't see everything you are doing?" he shifts, readjusting the growing bulge in his pants.

"Then you can listen."

I came up here and turned on a Christmas playlist before rejoining the party, and the chorus to 'Do You Hear What I Hear' echoes through the room just as I turn on the vibration feature on the wand, and I chuckle at the irony. Knox doesn't notice. His eyes become fixed on the toy in my hand as I lower it between my legs.

"Oh, shit," I moan as the vibration brushes across my clit. I've never felt a sensation quite like it. It's not something Knox could mimic if he tried. It's intense, different, and… Blake was right, fun!

As the pressure builds, it feels like the walls seem to close in on me inch by inch, as if the entire house is bracing for a snowstorm no one is prepared for. The lights outside the window are still twinkling, the melody of the music still soft in the background, but the surrounding air has turned brittle, cracking like logs on the fire. Every jingle of the song playing feels off key, every shadow stretched out long as I hold my breath in anticipation of release.

It might be the toy, the playful forbidden feeling of this game we are playing. It could even be the heightening of my senses from the drink we consumed, but regardless, it's all raw and new, and I love it.

Knox sits in the seat across from me, and he undoes his pants.

"Knox. What did I say?" I scold.

He huffs a groan of discomfort and places his hands back on his lap with a cocky ass grin on his face.

"You already got yours, baby. It's my turn," I remind him. My words are breathy and hard to release as the vibration builds pressure between my legs. This will not take long. The sensation is too new, too intense.

Without warning, the pressure builds, and a loud moan escapes my lips. My heart thunders in my chest, and my body quakes. I can feel my arousal pool as the climax hits me in shuttering wave after wave.

When I open my eyes, Knox is at the end of the bed, eyes full of heat and want.

"That was so fucking hot, Stitch."

He leans down and gives me a heated kiss to end the perfect high I'm coming down from.

Knox

THE SOUND OF VIBRATION fills the room. I was going to tell her we needed to scale this back so we could entertain our guests, but, fuck me. Telling her that would be like cutting my own legs out from underneath me. I walked into the room and saw her, wrapped in gold lace like a flame caught mid-flicker, glowing, untouchable and dangerously beautiful. The gold clung to her, accentuating every curve of her body, highlighting all of my favorite details.

Her skin is marked with stories, stretch marks like soft lightning, scars across her arms and chest like quiet battle cries. I can't stop touching them when I'm near her. Every line pulls me in deeper, proof of everything she's lived through, everything that makes her *real*. They aren't flaws, they're my Ana. Something in the way they are accentuated makes my breath hitch. I want to trace all of them with my fingers, with my mouth. She is gorgeous not despite them, but *because* of them. They make her the sexiest damn thing I've ever seen, and she knows it. While most women want to hide their scars, she wears them with a confidence unmatched by most.

"Oh, shit," she moans loudly as the vibration brushes across her clit.

Shifting in the seat, I undo my pants. I know we have guests downstairs. I know they are probably looking for me, realizing we are both missing. I'm sure there will be stares and wondering faces when we return, and still I couldn't give two fucks about what they think.

"Knox. What did I say?" she scolds me.

I huff a groan of discomfort and place my hands back on my lap with a cocky-ass grin on my face. I love when she bosses me around like this and she knows it.

"This is not about you," she reminds me. Her words are broken and seem caught in her throat as the vibration increases the pleasure between her legs. She shifts slightly and is now right on the edge of the bed. This will not take long. I can tell. The sensation is taking over her body.

Without warning, her legs quiver, a small sheen of sweat coats her skin, and a loud cry erupts from her lips. As she shifts her position again, she stretches too far, not in control of her motions as she comes and knocks over the snow globe on the corner the nightstand next to the bed. My heart thunders in my chest, and my body quakes right along with hers. She shutters, and I suddenly feel too far.

When she opens her eyes, I'm at the end of the bed, eyes full of heat and want.

"That was fucking hot, Stitch."

She smiles at me. "This is too much fun, baby." Her voice is low and satiated. "But we need to get back to all the guests."

"We do." My response is low. "I just want one more second to admire you like this."

She doesn't move, as if she's allowing me to freeze this vision in my brain, but that's not enough. I pull out my phone and quickly take a picture. "No one will see it. I'll put it in a hidden gallery," I promise her.

She doesn't flinch. She trusts me wholeheartedly.

"What's next?" I ask her, curious what else she has up her sleeve.

"Nothing until all our guests are gone. This little game is nowhere near over, baby. We're here for one more day." She stands and makes her way to the ensuite, and I bask in the sight of her hips swaying as she walks out of sight.

My phone pings, and the message on the screen sends an icy chill up my spine.

Marcus: Ummm… Your phone has been casting YouTube Christmas songs all night, right?

Fuck… Fuck… no, no, no, no. She's going to die.

Knox: Fuck, man. How many people saw the picture?

Marcus: Only a few. It flashed quickly.

Knox: Thanks for the heads-up.

I returned to the party, knots rolling like rocks in my stomach, and Ana emerged a few minutes later, a glow to her skin. Fuck, she's beautiful. Too bad I can't focus on that right now. I'm too busy playing interference, rushing around to every guest trying to get the awkward glances and side comments out of the way before she realizes what happened.

My phone pings again and my heart jumps. I look down to see a text from Cash, causing me to take a sigh of relief.

Cash: Not going to make it, man. I got stuck at a meeting with my PR manager for way too fucking long.

I shoot him off a text telling him not to sweat it, as I make my way over to Andrew and Larson, the foundation members who oversee Cash's volunteer work at the hospital. They have big cocky mouths, so I brace myself for the interaction.

"Hey," I say, placing my hands on Larson's shoulder. "Cash can't make it. He got stuck in a PR meeting."

"His team manager is a real douche," Larson responds. "He acts like Cash being the face of a youth athletic rehab centre is not good for the image of the entire Sun Cat's organization."

"How is it coming along?" I ask.

"Great! We should be ready to open up by summer," Adam answers with an enthusiastic tone.

"Man, I wish something like this was around when I had my injury. It would have saved me." I try to make sport of it, even though it's not funny. I'm never sure how to talk about my tangled past.

"It's why Cash partnered with us and brought it here. He's a good guy." Larson clearly admires Cash.

"He truly is one of the best guys I know." Even with the recent developments, and with Cash getting in a fight at Blake's opening, my impression of him stays the same. I am sure there is more to that story than we know but to me he is still one hell of a guy.

"Well, I hope you're enjoying yourselves," I say as I shake their hands.

"Not as much as you," Larson says with a wink.

There it is.

My head falls, and he pats me on the shoulder in a reassuring way. "Don't sweat it. Most of the people here were visiting and didn't even see it."

"Do you know who might have? I need to do damage control?" I plead.

"For sure, the two of us and that Marcus guy. No one else seemed to notice." Andrew's voice is calm and confident as he speaks to me.

"Let's hope so. Ana will be mortified." I shake my head, pissed that I could be so careless and put my wife in this situation.

I spent the next few hours entertaining guests, grazing on the buffet Ana created on the kitchen island, and enjoying the sight of my wife doing the same. All while hoping she has fun and doesn't find out about the incident until I tell her later.

Watching her and realizing how careless I was, I wonder what sparked the idea of this game. This is so unlike her. I mean, don't get me wrong, I fucking love it. I just hope she knows how much I love her, how perfect I think she is.

Fuck.

A knot forms in the pit of my stomach. Does she need more from me… sexually? Does Ana think we have a boring sex life?

I know we don't have sex as often as we'd both like to. The kids have become cockblock 1 and 2. But, shit. Am I neglecting her?

With that thought lingering in the back of my brain, I plot a little surprise of my own for her.

Not So Silent Night

"Makin' lots of noise on Christmas Eve, if you're not
having fun then you've gotta leave."
-Phil Vassar, Lonestar

Ana

T HE GUESTS ARE ALL gone now. The cottage is quiet, leaving me in nothing but my thoughts. Tonight has been so much fun. Blake was right. Games and toys do, in fact, make sex more interesting. I was hesitant. I mean, when we have sex, it's amazing, it's just lacking in frequency, but I guess that's expected in any marriage with two kids under 5. Neither of them are in school, and are still very dependent on the two of us. I like to think we have built a life full of love and balance. We share childcare responsibilities equally, neither one of us bears the sole weight of parenting, leaving us both completely exhausted. Our time away has been magical, rekindling the spark I've been longing for, but man, do I miss those two messy little faces. Knox briefly pulled me away to FaceTime them, but they were already snuggled in bed.

My mind shifts back to the man I love downstairs finishing up the dishes. I left Knox the last note for the evening in his jacket pocket, so I'm now just waiting for him, naked on the bed, to make his way up here.

No box, no bow, no wrapping in sight.

But your present's waiting, on this not so silent night.

It's not on a shelf, or under a tree,

Just follow the twinkle… and come find me.

-Stitch

When he appears in the doorway, tie undone, jacket slung over his shoulder, and a smirk on his face, I melt into the sheets.

"Stitch."

He breathes in sharply when he sees me, like he wasn't ready for the way I still get to him. That sound, simple and involuntary, lights something in me. Makes me feel wanted even with my body covered in scars and marks left behind from battles I've fought and carrying our two beautiful children. Even with all of that, he looks at me like I'm the most incredible thing he's ever seen. Like he can't believe I'm his. That's the magic. It's what gives me the strength to wear them like a badge rather than a suit of armor, not something to hide behind, but something to stand tall in.

Before I know it, he's at my side, his emerald eyes hungry as his gaze rakes across my exposed body. As he walks beside me he brushes his fingers over my skin, leaving goose bumps in their path from my waist, to my breasts, and then finally sliding them into my mouth. When my lips close around the pad of his middle finger, he lets out a quiet moan, and I know we are on the same page with how the night will end.

I watch as his eyes follow every curve of my body, and he slides his tie off. He leans down to kiss me and brings each hand over my head. The bed is king size, with wrought iron spindles decorating the head and footboard. I watch as he slides one end of the tie between the rungs and then uses it to fasten my wrists together over my head. My breath quickens and butterflies shoot through me as I lay vulnerable in front of him, full of anticipation.

"Spread your legs so I can see you," he demands.

I do as he says, letting my knees fall open to my sides, leaving me on full display. Only, he doesn't move where I want him. Instead, he backs up and moves to the foot of the bed. From there, I know he's getting a better look by the way his tongue darts out and his teeth move the metal of his lip ring back and forth. It's the telltale sign of his arousal, his need, every filthy desire he has. He slowly unfastens his belt and slides his pants off, immediately palming his hard erection. He pumps up and down as he watches me shift beneath his gaze.

"Imagine how good it will feel to have my mouth between those sexy legs, baby." He's taking his time. "How sweet it will be when your pussy squeezes every drop coming from my body."

"Touch me," I beg, but he doesn't move. He continues moving his hand up and down the length of his dick, while I watch each motion. It's as if my gaze is creating the friction he enjoys with each slow pass.

I lick my lips in response, wanting him in my mouth so bad at this moment.

"Come here." I try to move closer to the edge of the bed, but not making much headway with the way he has me tied up.

"You look good enough to fucking eat." Knox ignores my request and continues stroking himself, increasing his pace with every motion. I watch him, and my need for physical contact grows with each passing second.

"Knox." I tilt my head, begging and signaling for him to come closer.

I watch as he squeezes the head of his cock and then quickly removes his hand. He's edging himself.

In slow, deliberate strides, he moves to the edge of the bed next to me, placing a hand on my sensitive skin, running feather-like touches up and down my thigh. Each time his hand reaches the top of my leg, it dances across my opening with a ghostly presence.

"Mmmm," he groans. "You are fucking beautiful, Stitch."

He circles around my opening, and then changes his path down the length of my leg, repeating the pattern several times. With each pass, he gets closer to where I want him, to where I need him. This time, as he passes, I shift my hips slightly, causing his fingers to travel directly over my clit and the sensation is delicious.

"Oh, Knox. Please."

This time, he doesn't deny me. He slides his fingers in and out of me, bringing his mouth to my center and sucks my clit into his mouth, rolling it between his lips, matching the pace of his fingers. It's the best feeling in the world, pressure building, the tension ready to shatter like shards of glass at any moment. My hips rock, my walls tighten, and he withdraws his fingers and pulls away from me in one swift motion.

"No, no, no, no, no." The words tumble out of me faster than I can register his movement. "Knox."

My words are strained and painful. He's not only edged himself, he's edging me too. Before I know what he's doing, he climbs on top of me, lining himself with my entrance and pounding into me with a force that sends shivers up my spine.

"Oh, fuck." His words are rough and gravely. "You always feel so fucking good, baby."

"What does it feel like?" I ask, wanting to hear all the delicious details spill from his lips.

"The way you wrap around me… baby, it's unreal. So tight, so warm—I can feel you pulsing every time I move."

Erratic and rough. Those are the only words I can use to describe his motions at this moment. He moves in and out faster than his words can tumble out.

My walls clench, and again he pulls away from me, leaving me at the peak of build up, panting and needing nothing more than release.

I roll my hips against the air, seeking the friction he refuses to give. My thighs tremble, caught in the electric tension between want and willpower. Shit, he could end this in seconds. But he won't, because for him, it's not about the finish. It's about the ache. For me, it's the way my body begs, the way my mind spins with fantasies, *his* mouth, *his* voice, the weight of *his* gaze. It's delicious and too much all at once, and with the crackle of tension in the air between us, I pull hard against my restraint, wanting to tear the fabric to shreds, and then, he's inside me again, the sounds of skin slapping filling the room until a warm flood fills me, my strained screams bounce off the walls, and my body shakes in the aftershock of the most intense orgasm of my life.

We collapse, him still inside me. I don't know where my body ends and his begins. I don't want to.

Knox

I WAS DEEP IN a dream with snowflakes falling softly outside, Ana in red velvet, and something definitely involving whipped cream in a suspiciously empty room at a Christmas party. Things were just getting good. Her mouth hovered close to mine, carols playing somewhere in the background, and then I was startled by her phone vibrating like it had unresolved holiday trauma, tearing me away from my dream.

Bzzzz. Bzzzz.

I groan. Loudly.

Another buzz. I crack one eye open to see her phone lighting up in the dark room. "Ana," I mutter, half draped across the bed.

She doesn't move. Not even a twitch. Just keeps sleeping like the angel she is… with a devil of a device rattling on the table beside her.

Bzzzz. Again.

I roll over and blindly reach for the nightstand, missing it and smacking the lamp instead. The lights flash on, and I blink, trying to focus my vision.

Still nothing from her. She just curls toward me in her sleep, her cheek brushing my shoulder, one leg sliding across mine. Like I wouldn't notice. Low blow.

I peek at the screen: group chat. Again. Probably another round of Christmas memes or someone panic texting about a present they forgot. "You need new friends," I mutter. "Ones who don't text at 7 a.m."

Even as I say it, I smile. Because there she is, peaceful, warm, tangled up in our mess of flannel sheets and wearing fuzzy socks because her feet get cold.

She rubs her eyes. "Can you hand it to me?"

Reluctantly, I hand her the phone instead of pulling her onto my chest.

She shoots up with a giant smile on her face and frantically tries to find something to put on while simultaneously making a call.

"What are you doing?" My voice is groggy with sleep as I clutch the sheets where she was just curled up next to me. I just want to lay here, in bed, with my naked wife. Instead, I watch her bend over, giving me the perfect view of her ass, while she frantically throws items out of her suitcase, mumbling about finding her robe.

"Babe, it's in the bathro—" My words are cut short by the sound of Blake on the other end. Ana raises the phone and I quickly realize she's on FaceTime, hence the frantic shuffling trying to locate said robe.

"Show me!" are the only words I hear leave her mouth before April enters the call, shrieking with excitement.

"It's so pretty! I love the dark colors. It fits you perfectly." She pulls the phone closer to her face to get a better look at the screen.

"Damn, my brother did good," April giggles and their voices fade as Ana makes her way down the hall.

I let out a loud groan, knowing the second she gets coffee in her, and finishes what is about to be a *long* conversation with the girls, coming back to bed will be the last thing she is going to want to do.

Might as well get in the shower so we can go get breakfast. There is a little bakery in town I want to take her to. Apparently from what I hear, they have killer cinnamon rolls which are Ana's favorite.

"Luke proposed!" She comes back into the room with the biggest smile on her face.

Guess I read that wrong. My girl is full of surprises.

"That's great news! They're so great together." I offer her a smile as she walks my way. "Hey, I want to take you on a breakfast date." I tell her as she crawls back in bed next to me.

"That sounds fun. Where are we going?"

"There's a little bakery in town called Whisked Away. I heard they have killer cinnamon rolls and a toasted chestnut spiced vanilla latte I thought you might like. We can people watch and eat until we're uncomfortable."

Ana took her time getting ready while she FaceTimed the kids, getting distracted as Riker showed her all the fun holiday crafts he has been doing with Claire. Rory's still too young to make crafts, so he was super excited he got to make hers too.

The smell of cinnamon and peppermint fill the air as we walk into the bakery. This place is straight out of one of those Hallmark movies Ana loves so much.

Twinkling fairy lights wrap around the front porch giving it that golden glow that makes everything feel magical.

Inside, the wooden floors creak just enough to be quaint. There's a glass display case packed with red and green frosted cupcakes, flaky golden croissants, and seasonal pies topped with lattice crusts and sugared cranberries. Behind the counter is a chalkboard menu written in curly handwriting, with specials reading "Peppermint Chai Latte" and "Grandma Mae's Apple Cider Donuts."

People are gathering at vintage tables with mismatched chairs, sipping coffee from handmade mugs and catching up on what appears to be small town gossip. As if plucked right off the screen, there's even a golden retriever napping on the welcome mat, with a festive red and green collar.

"Knox, this is like a freaking dream." Her smile is so big and contagious I can't help but smile right back.

The Christmas music is soft as it plays through the speakers overhead while the staff are dressed to impress with their ugly Christmas sweaters. The sign by the host stand has large letters scrolled across it, 'Seat yourself, sugarplum,' which has Ana chuckling as she reads it.

"Where are we sitting, Stitch?" even though I already know the answer. There are two counter top tables in the middle of the bakery with cook stations in the middle, similar to hibachi, with diner stools surrounding it.

She looks at me with a huge smile, "The stools are all empty, and we'd have the best view in the house."

I gesture for her to lead the way, and I can't help but notice the slight pep in her step accompanied by an almost unrecognizable limp, not the kind you get from an injury, but the kind that makes my balls tighten.

Yep, I'm just cocky enough to know she'll be feeling me for days.

"Knox." She interrupts my thoughts with a light smack on the arm just as we take our seats. "Look at that cinnamon roll, it's almost the size of my head and looks so gooey."

"I told you they were supposed to be amazing."

Just then the waitress approaches, setting down a menu. Ana smiles up at her. "Oh, don't worry about the menu. We'll take two cinnamon rolls, and the best latte you've got."

Just as the words leave her mouth she turns to me and whispers like she's telling me a secret, "I've always wanted to do that."

"I know." I smile. Ordering 'the best' thing on the menu without knowing what it is she's getting is something she always wants to do, but for some reason can never build the courage to do. She usually chickens out and then panic orders every time, but something in her has shifted this weekend.

"What about you hun, what will you have to drink?" the waitress asks.

"I'll take a coffee, black. Thank you."

"You really think we're going to eat two of those things?" I ask, turning my attention back to Ana.

"No." She snorts a laugh. "But we can take it with us and eat it later."

"Okay, I thought maybe you've worked up an appetite with all of our activity," I tease.

"Oh, I have." She wiggles her brow.

"What do you think their story is, babe?" I gesture towards a couple sitting at a table by the window. He's reading the paper, and she's doing what appears to be a crossword puzzle. They both have white hair that shimmers in the sunlight peeking through the window, both wearing Christmas sweatshirts, sipping their coffee.

"They look like they met at a dance in high school. He was supposed to meet someone else, but walked in and saw her, immediately asking her to dance. Only he didn't like to dance, so his date was shocked when she walked in, leaving abruptly. They were so lost in each other's eyes they didn't even notice anyone else around them. It was love at first sight."

"That shit only happens in movies, Stitch."

"That's not true." She looks offended by my statement.

"Name one time someone walked into a room and instantly fell in love like the love sick sappy shit you see in romance movies."

"For real?" She grabs her phone and turns the screen towards me, my face appearing on the screen on her camera app. "Knox, meet the lovesick sap who fell hopelessly in love at a bar with a badass bitch who wanted nothing to do with him."

I just chuckle because she's right. I did that.

Let's Get Cozy

"Our love is something priceless…"

-Katie Perry

Ana

"So what exactly sparked this spicy little weekend?" he asks me as we walk up main street.

"What do you mean?" I slowly sip my latte, avoiding his gaze, because while I know exactly what he means, it's a conversation I don't want to have. How do I tell him I wish we had more time alone, more time to kindle the fire between us, to be like we used to be? All while explaining how I don't want a single thing in our current life to change. I love our kids and the life we have built, and wouldn't trade it for the world. He'll never understand. If I can't make it make sense in the secret corners of my brain where it lingers, there is no way I can make it make sense out in the world.

"Anabelle, you are a wonderful mother, an even more amazing wife. You're strong, you're stubborn as hell, and

I swear to God you never back down. That's what I love about you. There are a million ways I could describe you, but dense is not one of them, baby. Tell me what is going on."

"Why does something have to be going on?" I cringe as the words leave my mouth, because I know he sees right through me. I'm as transparent as a silk sheet blowing in the wind. Only my fibers are delicate and frail right now, instead of strong and binding. I pause for a moment and then admit, "You're right babe, I'm off. I would never entertain you dodging my questions." I swallow, trying to find the words lodged in my throat.

Where do I begin?

"Knox, I miss you. I miss us." I pause, drowning in thoughts I can't hold onto long enough to name, each one slipping through my fingers before I can say it aloud.

"Baby, we see each other every day. I make sure I'm home from the facility early so I can help with dinner, laundry, and bath time. I try so hard to maintain as much normalcy in our schedule that being a business owner will allow." His eyes are glassy, and I recognize the defeat in his eyes. He thinks he's letting me down, letting us down, which is precisely why I wanted to avoid this conversation.

"No, Knox, look at me. When it comes to husbands, having a partner in all the craziness, I married the real life Jack Fucking Pearson. It's just, we went from being buried in the sheets coated in sweat to buried under piles of laundry and toys coated in leftover remnants of breast milk. We lay next to each other at night, and more often than not, leaning over to lay my head on your chest feels like a marathon I haven't trained for. I miss walking in the door and wanting nothing more than your dick in my mouth. I fantasize about waking up to coffee and an orgasm. It's a good fucking morning if at least one of us gets to drink our coffee while it's hot. Fuck," I moan so loud a couple walking past forget they're pretending not to listen to our conversation. "I miss hot coffee so fucking much I almost came in the middle of the bakery."

The woman giggles as she passes and whispers confirmation to her husband that she remembers feeling the same way. "They must have little kids." Her smile is so warm and sympathetic it makes me feel so fucking seen.

"I love my dick in your mouth. I love my dick in your mouth, your hand, your pussy, your ass," he whispers the last part with a cheeky smile. "But fuck, Stitch, sometimes my love for those things just doesn't compare to my unrelenting desire for sleep."

I belly laugh, one that courses through my entire body. I feel it deep in my soul. "Samesies."

"Riker's new favorite word rubbing off on you?" His question is accompanied by a melodic chortle, my favorite sound in the world.

"It sounds cuter when he says it." I smile.

"It is." He confirms as he wraps me in a hug with his chin resting on top of my head. "I'm sorry Riker and Rory are the two neediest little cock blocks around."

"Shit, they really are. Oh! Let's call them CB1 and CB2. We can even make them little red shirts with white letters, you can dress like The Cat in the Hat and I'll be Carols K. Krinklebein, for Halloween. We will be the cutest family on the block."

"Why do you get to be the grumpy fish?"

"Are we really going to argue over who gets to be the grumpy fish?" I ask, amused by where this conversation has led us.

"Yes, we are. Because I know you're serious, and both of the kids are terrified of the fish, which means you don't have to carry them and all the fucking candy. Rory already hates the stroller, and if she's anything like her brother, she'll want nothing to do with being restrained when candy is involved."

"How about we worry about who will be the fish in 10 months, and tonight you focus on all the places you'd love to have your dick?"

Knox

As much as Ana wants me to focus on the places I love to have my dick, I want to focus on her, adore her, pamper her. Plus I need a little time away from her to process my fuck up at the party and think through how I'm going to tell her what happened.

Being away from the kids creates opportunities for us sexually that we don't have at home, and fuck I love it. But it also creates opportunities for her to relax, and focus on herself, a privilege she rarely gets the opportunity to exercise at home.

"Stitch," I whisper against her neck as she pours a glass of wine in the kitchen. She hums in response, and the vibration of the noise against my lips is delicious. "I drew you a bath upstairs."

She turns in my direction and I can't read the expression, it's one I have never seen. I thought I'd memorized every pattern, every expression, but this one. It's new. Her expression is frozen in place: wide eyes, parted lips caught somewhere between surprise and an emotion I can't quite decipher. Her unreadable emotion lingers on her face like a snapshot on a camera, suspended mid frame.

"Stitch." My voice, though soft, snaps her out of her motionless stance, and she starts crying. Tears fall from her eyes in pools. "Fuck, what's wrong?"

"You drew me a bath? I told you I wanted to suck your dick and put it in all my holes, and you drew me a bath?" Her words are ones that when put together in this context should sound sarcastic, laced with irritation. Instead, they are soft and have a hint of warmth to them. It only adds to my confusion.

"Yes?" My response is a question, not a statement. There is not one ounce of confidence in my voice. I'm not quite sure how to play this. "Are you upset? I wanted to—"

She doesn't wait for me to finish, she grabs her wine and heads up the stairs to the master suit. She absentmindedly discards articles of clothing as she glides through the cottage, and I'm a little scared to follow her. Is she getting in the tub enraged? Are we about to hate fuck?

I mean that could be fun, we haven't done that… well ever.

She walks into the bathroom and gasps. I know what caught her by surprise. The bathroom is dark, with white Christmas lights I took off the railings and scattered along the counters and floor creating a warm soft glow in the bathroom. There is one small candle on the edge of the tub that I found on a shelf in the living room. I placed her kindle on the wood tray that sits across the tub along with a few little snacks, and have my phone on the counter playing instrumental Christmas music.

She cries… Again. Shit. Only this time, it's more of a sob. She discards her lace panties and steps into the tub, setting her wine on the tray as she sinks beneath the water.

Her tits float perfectly above the warm liquid that surrounds her, I have to blink a few times and adjust the boner forming in my pants as I squat down next to her.

I'd grabbed one of her clips from the counter and placed it on the tray so she could pull her hair up. I reach for it, place it in between my teeth as I whisk her hair away from her face, and pull her wet ends on top of her head and then fasten it in place with the clip.

She smiles through her tears and readjusts her hair. "Thank you, that was so romantic, but it was kind of floppy."

I pull her chin in my direction and her eyes are on mine, "Why are you crying?"

"All I wanted to do was fuck you in every way possible, as many times as possible all weekend. I made you filthy delicious promises, and all you want to do is pamper me. Your dick was painfully hard in the car all the way home, you're hard right now, Knox, and still all you want to do is pamper me."

"Yes," I respond to confirm her thinking. Even though I'm still not quite sure what it means.

"Knox, I offered for you to fuck my ass, and you made me a bath, with a boner. You ignored your boner for me, to do something for me. That's true love."

I laugh, "That's true love?"

"Yes. Do you know how many guys would have just railed me? Just ignored the signs of my exhaustion, how defeated I get by all the things. Knox, as much as I want to rekindle our sex life, I fucking needed this. I needed this and didn't even know it." She smiles. "But you did."

Oh, thank fuck.

I kiss her on the forehead and stand. "You stay here until your hands and feet are pruney and the water is cold. I'll make dinner, keep it warm, and when you get in bed, text me, and I'll bring it up here, where we can have dinner in bed.

"Knox Reed, I fucking love you. I've never had dinner in bed, but it sounds better than breakfast in bed. Now leave me the fuck alone so I can soak."

"Now you want to soak? That's not something I have the restraint for, Stitch." I wink and leave her to relax, but her laugh follows me out of the room. I love every second of it.

Now to process how the fuck to tell her what I did without also making her think it's the reason I drew her bath… fuck! It just gets more and more complicated the longer I put it off.

White Christmas

"I'm dreaming of a white Christmas"

-Michael Buble, Shania Twain

<h1 style="text-align:center">Ana</h1>

"**O**H MY GOD," I moan so loud my chest vibrates. "This is amazing."

"You *look* amazing," Knox teases.

I look over at him with my Italian sub in my hand, mouth full of delicious meat and give him my best grin.

"Mind your business, Knox. I'm having a moment here with my sandwich."

"You're making noises over there that are making it hard for me to focus on my own sandwich. You're makin' me hard, Stitch."

"Don't you fucking dare interrupt this dinner in bed experience. Do you know the last time either of us actually finished our food in one sitting?" I push him away as he attempts to lean in for a kiss, blocking him with a huge bite of my grinder. "This is the best thing I've ever had in my mouth."

"That's fucking rude," Knox says with a snicker. "But yeah, samesies." I scrunch my nose in dislike of his use of the word.

"Nope. You're right," I laugh. "That is Riker's coined phrase and should remain that way. It's only cute coming from him."

Knox and I sit in bed eating our subs and chips while gulping down Diet Coke in absolute silence, and it is magical. It really is the best meal I have had in a long time. Once the last bite is gone, Knox doesn't waste any time.

As soon as all the food is gone, his lips are on mine. He pushes me back onto the bed making me giggle.

"What's so funny?" He curls a brow.

"We're literally going to be rolling in crumbs. I can feel them sticking to me already."

"Guess I'll have to lick them off of you then." He deepens our kiss, and the second our tongues meet, I melt into him. The taste of him, any part of him, on my tongue is my favorite. The feel of his soft lips caressing mine makes me go feral, placing a small bite on his lip ring.

Both of us shimmy out of our clothes like this is the only time we will get to be like this, and in some ways, it might be, at least for a while.

As soon as his cock springs free and his erection bounces in front of me, I want nothing more than to lick the bead of precum forming on his tip. I want to be more than the mom of his children, I want to make his darkest desire come true.

I start at his balls and lick my way from the base to tip, moaning when the salty flavor meets my tastebuds. Like I said, his taste is my favorite. With one swift motion, I slide him into my mouth until he meets the back of my throat causing it to constrict. I close my mouth around him and suck hard repeatedly, using my tongue to message the underside of his hard length. He wraps his hands around the back of my head with a moan and fucks my face with a furious pace.

This, right here is what's been missing.

I look up at him through watery eyes, and the sight of him coming undone takes my breath away.

I have memorized this sight, and still, it captivates me every time. The veins in his forearms bulge, pressing against his tight skin, matching the ones that are being rubbed in my mouth, begging to be released from the tension. His breaths become ragged, causing his chest to rise and fall, increasing in pace with each inhalation. His eyes are closed, and he rolls his lip ring between his teeth. If I had to pick one thing that gets me, it's that.

Goosebumps break out over his skin, the telltale sign that he's about to explode. As soon as I see them scatter across his skin, hot liquid spirits down my throat, and I swallow every single drop, waiting until he comes down from the high to pull him out of my mouth and wipe the remnants of saliva from my swollen lips.

Taking him in my mouth is always raw and messy. I can't put it into words but it's something I love too much.

"Get on your hands and knees and show me that ass," Knox demands.

I do as he says, propping my elbows on a pillow.

"Look at that sweet ass. I wish you could see what you look like dripping for me, with your tight rippled hole begging for me." He spits and then spreads it with his thumb over the entrance before pushing his thumb inside. The sensation makes my toes curl, but I'm distracted by the thought of him admiring my ass in the air, his thumb rolling over my opening.

"You don't want to use your phone to show me?"

"No." He pauses for a brief second before returning to mission, worshiping me.

"I thought that was going to be our new thing, you taking pictures of me."

Again, he stills for a second. It's barely noticeable but my words clearly interrupted the cadence of him sliding in and out of me. I'm probably imagining things.

"What's in that box?" he asks, referring to the little gold box sitting on the nightstand.

I open the small note on top, a box I left there this morning as a part of the game we've been playing. I had planned on leaving it on the kitchen counter for him, but the pampering changed plans, so I brought it here, hoping it would spark his curiosity. This is something I know he's wanted to explore, so I know he'll love it.

I unfold the little piece of paper and hold it up for him to see.

I'm dreaming of a white Christmas, but not the kind with snow. Instead I'll be waiting with mistletoe in nothing but a bow.

Next I open the box, and inside is some booty bling with a rhinestone bow at the end. Beneath it is a remote and small vial of lube.

A sly smile spreads across his face, and he silently slips the plug and lube from the box. I watch him over my shoulder as he examines it, before popping open the lube and coating the end. He takes the remaining liquid and coats me with it, inserting one finger, and then two and slowly rolling them in circles to make room for the plug.

"Knox," I moan just as he slips his fingers back out, and the empty feeling from where his fingers had been is replaced by the soothing feel of the cool metal. I moan at the sensation as he slowly moves it in and out until it fits inside me.

"Fuck, this is beautiful." His voice is dripping with heat.

"I want to see it, Knox."

He hesitates before reaching for my phone and clicking a picture to show it to me.

"The bow is beautiful," I breathe as he turns on the vibration.

"Your ass is beautiful, all decorated like the best Christmas present," he says looking at the picture for a moment.

He positions himself behind me and slowly slides the head of his dick into my soaking pussy.

"Shit! You are so wet, baby. I love how ready you are for me all the time. It's so sexy."

"Knox, please fuck me. Hard." My voice is coated with urgency and desire.

He does just as I ask, slamming into me over and over again.

"Fuck, baby. I can feel the plug each time I thrust... shit, it feels so fucking good."

He finds the perfect rhythm and continues until we are both a sweaty mess, and the walls of my pussy clench around him. I collapse on the bed while he pulls the plug out of me and walks to the bathroom. I hear the water run and watch him open the shower and retrieve the soap. After a few minutes he returns with the red shimmery bow glistening in the dim light. He props me up, placing a pillow under my hips, takes the rest of the lube from the vial and strokes his cock with it. Once every delicious inch is covered, he lines up with my ass and slides inside.

"Oh," I moan.

"Relax baby. I'm barely in but I want to fill this ass with my come."

"I'm trying, but I feel like I'm going to come again."

"Good," he says as he reaches for the wand I left on the nightstand, turns it on, and runs it over my clit. The walls of my core tighten, and I tremble at the sensation.

"That's it baby," he says as he slides the rest of the way in. "Hold this here," he encourages me as he transfers it from his hand to mine over my clit.

The vibration is smooth and consistent. A sensation that could not be replicated, and I welcome the new feel as Knox pumps in and out of me. After a few calculated shifts of his hips, along with the vibration, I fall over the edge, screaming his name. I don't know what it is about him in my ass, but it sends me reeling every single time. A toe curling, heart racing, sweat beading release.

I reach between my legs and massage his balls, knowing that's all it will take. Two more pumps and Knox spills into me with my name roaring on his lips.

"Just a little jingle of the balls and you fall over the edge?" I tease. "I'm good."

"You want a prize?" he jokes.

We sit and laugh for a few more minutes, and I decide this is the version of us I love the most. Playful and free.

Knox

"Hey baby." I feel my voice shake as the words leave my lips. I have to tell her. I have my phone open to the picture I took of her, rolling my fingers over the image in contemplation. We are so good right now. This could ruin it.

"You look beautiful in these pictures." My voice is betraying me as I try to dodge the conversation I just started.

Don't chicken out, you fucker. She is your wife. You don't keep secrets, I silently scold myself.

Ana turns towards me as she rinses the shampoo from her hair in the shower. Her eyes are closed, but I recognize the concern sitting behind her lids.

"What's wrong?"

"Nothing." *Fucker.*

I take a second to gather my thoughts before deciding to face the fear deep in the pit of my stomach… the fear of disappointing my favorite person. "So, Marcus sent me a text at the party to confirm that my phone was casting YouTube on the TV playing Christmas music."

Her eyes shoot open. "When?"

"After I saved the picture I took of you."

"Knox." Her voice is low as her head tilts in question. "Everyone saw it?"

"No. Only Marcus and the two guys from the foundation."

"How do you know?" The tone in her voice is one I have never heard before.

"They assured me it flashed quick and no one else saw it."

"Ok." She returns to rinsing her hair as if this conversation never happened, leaving me completely dumbfounded.

"Ana!" I shout in confusion.

"What?" she cackles in response.

"Why aren't you freaking out?"

"It happened. I can't change it. Only three people saw it, and I won't have to see them very often. Plus, the bitches who eye-fuck you and size me up didn't see it, thank fuck."

"You're not mad?"

"Not unless you did it on purpose." She laughs, she actually laughs while I'm over here freaking out.

"Knox, my body's been through so much, and I've worked hard to feel at home in it. I wear it with pride, partly because of you. You make me feel sexy, and that makes everyone else's opinions irrelevant."

I fall in love with her more every damn time she opens her mouth. She is unapologetically herself, so it would be pointless to continue the conversation. She's good, we're good, so I'm good.

"What time do you want to leave tomorrow morning, Stitch?" I ask, hoping she won't be in too big of a rush.

She grabs her towel and wraps it around her body. "Never." She smiles. "Knox, I love the fuck out of our kids, but I miss sleep and sex and hot food. Is it terrible of us to take our time and wait until we absolutely have to be out of here to leave?"

"Hell no. They'll never know. To be honest, they won't even remember we left."

"I was hoping you'd say that." She smiles.

"I'll go pop some popcorn, and you pick a movie." I usher her closer to the bed.

As I place the popcorn in a bowl, I smile at the picture our nanny sends us of Riker and Rory snuggled in bed. Then I grab two sodas and head up the stairs.

Ana is in the bed under a fluffy white blanket, fuzzy socks peeking out and my hoodie wrapped around her. The sight alone makes me so damn happy, but the movie on the screen is the cherry on top.

"How did you know I'd want to watch The Nightmare Before Christmas?"

"Funny. You act like we just met," she taunts.

I tear off my clothes and climb in bed next to her in only my boxers, bracing for the human furnace I'm about to cuddle with.

Ana plays the movie and my mind drifts back to when we met. I thought I loved her then, but shit, I had no idea what loving her really would be like in the long run.

Jingle Bell Cock

"Rockin' around the Christmas tree"

-Snowdrift Sleighs

<h1 style="text-align:center">Ana</h1>

"Mmmm." Hints of warm sugar and something yeasty and freshly baked fill the room. I turn over to reach for Knox, but the bed is cold.

"Knox," I yell from where I am buried under the covers, not quite ready to leave the warmth of the bed.

I hear him in the distance, and moments later he comes sauntering into the room with a plate in one hand, and a cup of coffee in the other. His muscles are perfectly taut beneath the veins in his arms, and his chest is covered in a light sheen of sweat. He was clearly working out in the gym downstairs this morning. There is no fucking way I'd ever join him, but damn do I love the sight of him after he exerts himself.

"Whatcha got there?" I ask sitting up a little taller to see over the edge of the plate.

"I got up a little early so I could run to the bakery to get a cinnamon roll before my workout. I had it warming in the oven." He smiles. "I know the smell is your favorite."

"It is." I smile back at him, loving how well he knows me. "Do you remember the last time you brought a dessert into the bedroom?" I wiggle my eyebrows suggestively.

"Fuck." He grins, pulling his lip ring in between his teeth and rolling it back and forth softly. "Yeah, and we never got the stain out of those sheets."

With one swift motion he places the plate on the nightstand next to me and crawls into bed on top of me.

The kiss he gives me is deep, demanding and rough. He increases the speed and intensity of his motions with every pass of his lips. When he moves from my mouth to my neck he begins to trace little circles with the tip of his tongue. I feel goose bumps pepper my skin.

My husband is a lot of things. He's a great father, an amazing business owner, selfless, motivated, loving beyond measure, but the way he claims me, making dirty little promises as he worships me, from the bend of my knee to the curve of my hipbone, that's my favorite version of him. Probably because it is quite literally the only side of him reserved just for me. The side no one else in the world is privileged enough to see.

There is a string of Christmas lights wrapped around the headboard and Knox pauses as he eyes them purposefully. Before I know it or have time to process his intention, he is unraveling them from the metal bedframe and securing them around my wrist, slightly tangling them around my body before he sits back and traces the path of the lights like a masterpiece he created from scratch. The cord stretches from wrist to wrist and his approval of his work is clear in his gaze.

"Fuck," he whispers, barely loud enough for the word to reach my ears. He begins playing with his damn lip ring again before he returns his lips to my body, kissing me starting at my toes and slowly cascading kisses up my entire body until he lays one soft kiss on my forehead.

My eyes trace every curve of his hard muscles, the light pattern of hair on his chest. The stubble on his chin scratches just enough to remind me of the first time he kissed me after skipping a shave—we were in the car, parked behind the old grocery store, and I didn't give a damn that my lips were raw for hours after. Knox is nothing short of breathtaking.

"Knox, my cinnamon roll is getting cold," I whisper.

"We haven't even done anything yet, and you already have an appetite?"

"Knox, that cinnamon roll started seducing me before you even got it out of the oven, and now it's just taunting me there, along with my coffee that's going cold." I laugh.

As he continues to kiss me, he peels off a small piece of the gooey roll and slides it between my lips. My teeth sink into the pillowy dough as the buttery sugar melts on my tongue. It's sweet and salty, with a hint of spice from the cinnamon invading my taste buds as a hint of vanilla lingers in the background.

"What am I going to do at home when I have just regular ass cinnamon rolls?" A small giggle escapes me, but he ignores me and continues kissing my body.

Without saying a word he dips his finger into the icing and paints each of my nipples white. He continues covering my skin as he kisses up and down my neck.

"You're making quite a mess," I joke.

"I'll clean it up, trust me. There will not be a speck of frosting left when I'm done with you." The smile he gives me is heated and full of sex.

He dips his finger back into the icing and begins to paint across my chest. When I look down a few seconds later, the word *mine* sits right above my breasts and he is quick to snap a picture before licking it clean.

"Mmmm. You are fucking delicious, Stitch."

"You think so?" I giggle.

"I absolutely know so. You are my favorite flavor." He begins at my jawline laying his tongue flat and slowly licks every trace of icing from my skin. Then as he finds places where the frosting is a little more reluctant to leave my skin, he gently sucks until there is nothing left.

Just when I think he's had enough, he removes the lights and flips me over so I'm propped on all fours before placing little pieces of the cinnamon roll down my back leading to my ass. He traces the path with his mouth like breadcrumbs leading him to a treasure.

His breath is warm, a whisper on my skin, and the feel of his tongue is soft and soothes the little nips he leaves in his path. The sensation causes little quakes between my legs in anticipation.

"Knox," I pant.

"Stitch," he calls back to me, his voice laced with lust. He brings his palm down on my ass and a squeal leaves my mouth just in time for him to repeat the motion.

"Oh, fuck," I moan. I feel every muscle in my body, even my pussy, clench in response. "I have something for you." My words are soft as I speak over my shoulder with a wiggle of my brow. He is obviously trying to make sense of the words I just spoke, wondering, filling his eyes.

Knox

"JINGLE BELL COCK," I say the words aloud as I read the tiny little package Ana just handed me. "Of all the things you could name something you expect me to wear on my dick…"

"Read the description. It's the best part." Her laughter fills the room and my breath hitches as I take her in, a carefree look in her eyes that are illuminated by the string of lights sprawled on the bed. I didn't secure them to restrain her, they're just for visual effect, and they are fulfilling that order as they reflect a soft glow on her skin.

"The Jingle Bell Cock ring wraps him in a soft stretchy holiday hug, complete with a festive red and white trim and just enough gold bells to make his spirits *very* bright. Slip it on and let the low rumbling vibes send him straight to the nice list, with an optional warming feature for cold winter nights." I quirk a brow, but fuck, for her, I'll try just about anything.

"What else do you have up your sleeve, Stitch?"

"This is my last surprise." She smiles. "Some just for fun, and some we can take home with us to keep the fun going all year round.

"Oh yeah, my dick decorated like a Christmas tree will be just what we need all year," I quip.

"Come on, it will take us well into the New Year, we can hang a love knot from it on Valentines day, dangle a little pot of gold from the gold balls on St. Patrick's Day, paint your balls like Easter eggs with edible paint, it might make you shoot come like fireworks for the 4th of July, it's a great Halloweenie costume… I mean who doesn't want Christmas on Halloween, plus it's my favorite snack for Thanksgiving, and then we're back at Christmas time."

I burst out laughing harder than I have in a long time. Ana can literally make everything make sense when it shouldn't. Even when she's joking.

"Ok you convinced me," I say as I slide the ring around my cock.

"It's so cute." Her smile is contagious.

"Don't you ever refer to my dick as cute ever again Anabelle. It's going to do unspeakable things to you that can't be called cute."

"So tough," she teases. "I'm sorry. I can't take you seriously with your dick all decked out."

"You're going to pay for that little jab," I promise as I pull her to the edge of the bed.

I push the little button on the side, and fuck me. The vibrations feel amazing.

I line myself up with her entrance, and she reaches between her legs and pushes the little button on the opposite side. A few seconds later, my balls begin to warm. It's not an intense feeling, but mixed with the vibration and the heat of her pussy as I slide inside her, I see fucking stars.

"Holy shit," I pant.

"Mmm… this feels, oh, shit!" Her words are erratic and fragmented. Sharp. Each syllable shatters before they reach the air. "Knox," she moans. My name barely makes it out, half breath, half sound, and fuck, it destroys me.

I slowly move in and out, worried that any faster pace will send me toppling over the edge before I can fully enjoy the moment.

She grinds her hips against me, pulling me closer with each pulse of my hips. We stay in the rhythm for several minutes before the need for friction builds to impossible heights. She flips over and pushes a pillow underneath her hips.

"Knox, I need you to fuck me… hard. Like some slut you just met and brought home for the night."

Those words are all it takes for my resolve to diminish. I stop holding back. No teasing. No pacing. Just fucking. Just heat, and sweat, and my cock driving into her like I've got hours left to make her forget her own name.

"Shut up and take my dick, Ana."

"Mmmm," she moans in approval of my brash tone.

"You fucking like it, I know you do. So fucking wet," I taunt as I slam into her.

My hips smack into her ass, the sounds of her arousal around my dick and skin slapping fill the room, mixed with the aroma of cinnamon, sugar and sweat. It's the most sinful smell I've ever known. Sweet, musky, human.

Suddenly she flips around, pushing me onto my back.

"I'm going to ride you until I come, Knox. I need you to lay there like a good boy and watch my tits bounce." Her voice is rough and gravely.

"Fuck, baby."

The lights perfectly illuminate her hair as she builds until she shutters around me, and I fall with her into a pleasure pool of our own making.

Walking in a Winter Wonderland

"Later on we'll conspire, as we dream by the fire"

-Laufey

Ana

"**H**I BABY!" RIKER IS jumping up and down on the other end of the FaceTime call.

"You coming home?" His voice is high pitched and full of excitement as he gives me a visual whiplash of the entire house, running from room to room with the phone in his hand, yelling nonstop until I manage to interrupt him.

"We sure are! We will be home in a few hours. I'll see you soon," I reassure him as I blow him a kiss and hang up.

"You hung up already." Knox seems a little disappointed I hung up so fast.

"It was like being on the world's most chaotic roller-coaster. He was running around the house not even talking, just screaming and attempting to show me all the decorations we hung before we left," I reassure him.

"Well, we better hurry home then." He smiles, after biting on his lip ring, taunting me.

"Did you get all the bathroom stuff?" I ask.

"Yes, and I looked under the bed, in the fridge, and took out all the trash."

"What about all the toys?" My voice is strained as I try to whisper as if there is anyone else here to hear me.

"Ana, I got all of it. I checked the cottage three times. If you're worried, why don't you go check it while I load the car." His voice is coated with his annoyed-husband tone.

"No, I trust you." I smile.

"Do you?" He smirks in response.

"You're such a smart ass sometimes."

"Well you're kind of a pain in my ass sometimes. The perfect passenger princess who questions all the things you don't want to do."

"You're damn lucky I decided to be your passenger princess. You almost missed out." My voice breaks at the thought.

"True," he says, pressing a kiss to my temple. "Do you want me to go do one more sweep?"

"No, let's go home."

The drive home was beautiful, but there is nothing quite as breathtaking as the sight of our cozy little house.

I worked so hard to turn this little house into a home for Riker and I, and Knox helped make it even more amazing after he moved in. He transformed it into a picture perfect vision, and it only gets better at Christmas time. As we drive up the world outside feels like it's holding its breath.

It's probably just me holding my breath.

Snow clings to the tree branches, the porch is dusted white with just enough snow that it crunches under our feet as we make our way up the steps. I giggle at the new doormat Knox found before we left that reads, *Home…
Finally.* The air right outside the door smells of pine and

chimney smoke with a faint aroma of something baking, kinda like gingerbread maybe, or something with nutmeg.

Spending the weekend rediscovering ourselves, just the two of us truly was magical, but nothing matches the feeling of coming home.

I reach for the door to open it, but Knox pulls me into his chest off to the side of the front door, where we are out of sight.

"What is it?" I ask, his expression is unreadable.

"I just want to steal one more second with you." He nestles me into the crook of his neck and rests his chin on the top of my head.

"Babe, we are going inside together. We both live here." I chuckle.

With his chin still resting on my hair, he whispers, "You know, the second we walk in there we are back to being busy parents scheduling sex, running ragged, falling into bed with barely enough energy to pull the covers up to fall asleep. So, I need you to hear something from me before the craziness steals the moment."

"Okay." I breathe in a heavy breath.

"Stitch, when I met you, I knew I loved you. I knew you were it for me. I really enjoyed this weekend away with you, exploring new sides of our relationship. I need you to know that I am so full of joy and happiness with what we have built together. What we had this weekend was love, lust and desire all mixed into one, and we need that sometimes. But what we have everyday, that's also love. True love that tells a story for the ages."

He gives me a kiss on the forehead making sure I know he means it.

"Love isn't like the movies. Love doesn't show up in the moments you tear each other's clothes off, it doesn't even show up in dramatic gestures, or romantic dates. That's where it starts though. When you love someone enough you put in the extra effort just to see them smile."

He uses the crook of his finger so my gaze meets his bright green one.

"Stitch, love shows up in the little moments, the ones you could blink and miss if you're not looking for them." His voice cracks and it breaks me.

"True love to me is stolen glances across the dinner table, passing touches that linger as we chase the kids around. Squeezing in behind you and the kids when you cuddle on the couch, just so I can touch you."

He steps back. Paces. Drags a hand over his jaw.

"It's a random phone call where we have nothing to say, and stay on anyway. It's making sure you have gas in your car so you never have to smell it on your fingers, making you cinnamon rolls even though I don't eat them. It's all the tiny moments that stretch between the big ones. Because fuck, if the little moments feel this good, the big ones are going to be heartstopping."

We have had such a fun weekend, and I don't want that to go away, but he's right, we have a whole life waiting for us on the other side of the front door, and it is magic. I look between Knox and the window, torn between two halves of my heart. I want to stay here with him just as much as I want to run inside.

"But fuck," his voice picks up again, making the decision a little easier, "love, lust and desire need to make a more regular appearance for us, because it's fun to date you again." He pauses, and I look him in the eyes as a tear falls down his cheek.

"Knox," I tilt my head and place both palms on his cheeks, pulling him in for a kiss.

"I can't lose you," he breathes out.

"What?" I shake my head in confusion.

"I love you so much every day, but I stopped dating you, enough that you were worried about the state of our sex life, enough to create this entire weekend of fun, and it never even occurred to me things had shifted."

"That's okay," I reassure him

"Fuck that! No, it's not. I should have noticed. I should have been the one to make a grand gesture this weekend, but I'm so fucking tired all the time it didn't even occur to me, you deserve better than that, I promised you I'd be better than that."

I smile at him, knowing my words will not be taken out of context with him. "Then be better, baby, don't get all in your head about it. If you *want* to be better, then be better. But not for me. I hit the jackpot with you. What if I want to romanticize you every once in a while? What if I want to remind you of all the dirty little reasons you're filled with lust and desire? This is a two-way street, Knox."

He pulls me back into his chest and wraps me in a hug. "Okay."

We stand here for a few minutes before deciding to go inside, stealing a few more seconds together before we settle back into life.

Christmas Morning

Knox

Anabelle,

There are very few things in this world that are certain, but the one thing that has always made sense to me, is you. Our life. Our kids.

I have done a lot of dreaming about our weekend away and it was fucking amazing. Then, to be honest, it pissed me off. I never thought we'd need a reset. A rekindling. But we did, and fuck, baby, I loved every second of it.

We are never going to need it again. I'm making a promise to you today that no matter what life throws at us, I will love you all day and devour you at night.

Before you come downstairs, I want you to take a bath, and drink the coffee I left for you—it's still hot thanks to the mug warmer I found. Yeah, I'm that guy now.

Oh, and I also got you a Christmas present that will last all year.

Starting after the new year, Hadley will be taking the kids one night a week for us to have a date night, and every three months… we get a weekend away.

I'm not waiting until next Christmas to have more fun.

-Knox

P.S. There is a little red iridescent envelope on the bathroom counter. You're not the only one with plans.

Acknowledgments

CREATING A CHRISTMAS STORY is a bit like baking a holiday pie, it takes time, care, and a whole lot of love. I couldn't have done it without some incredible people who supported me along the way!

My husband is my greatest gift. His patience, encouragement, and belief in me is what keeps me going. Thank you for cheering me on through late night writing sessions and early morning edits.

Words could not express the amount of love I have for my Beta team! Heather Newsome, Evelyn Charles, Lindsey Kelley, Sarah Peake, Kristina Jarman, Chrissie Goss, and Kelly McNair: your time, insight, and encouragement helped bring this story to life. Each of you brought something special to the process, and I'm so grateful.

JJ, you are the true magic that makes it all happen! Thank you for sifting through the weeds when I make changes and they don't quite make sense. Your attention to detail is unmatched, and you are a true gift!

And you—yes you! The readers. Thank you for choosing to spend part of your holiday season with Knox and Ana. Whether you are curled up on the couch with a cup of cocoa, or hiding from loved ones in a quiet corner, I hope this book brings you a little bit of the Christmas magic we all believe in.

It takes a village, and I am beyond blessed with mine! Wishing each of you a warm holiday season filled with joy, magic, and a little bit of spice.

Love,

Harper Rae